THE TECHNOLOGY OF
ANCIENT ROME

Charles W. Maynard

The Rosen Publishing Group, Inc., New York

APR **1 9** 2006

*This book is in memory of Mrs. Ann Romick, my first Latin teacher
and a dear friend, who introduced me to ancient Rome.*

Published in 2006 by The Rosen Publishing Group, Inc.
29 East 21st Street, New York, NY 10010

First Edition

Library of Congress Cataloging-in-Publication Data

Maynard, Charles W. (Charles William), 1955–
The technology of ancient Rome / Charles W. Maynard.
    p. cm.—(The Technology of the ancient world)
Includes bibliographical references and index.
ISBN 1-4042-0556-X (library binding)
1. Technology—Rome—History—Juvenile literature. 2. Rome—Civilization—Juvenile literature.
I. Title. II. Series.
T16.M394 2005
609.37—dc22

              2005013902

Manufactured in the United States of America

On the cover: Top: This ancient Roman stone roller mill, called a trapetum, was used to crush olives and was turned by men pushing the wooden handles while walking around the deep stone basin. The crushing mill is housed at the Antiquarium Museum in Pompeii, Italy. Bottom: An engraving from 1911 by J. Hoffbauer depicts the artist's impression of what the west side of the Roman forum would have looked like in the fourth century AD.

CONTENTS

INTRODUCTION: ROMAN TECHNOLOGY
   CONQUERS THE WORLD 4

1 THE TECHNOLOGY OF AGRICULTURE AND TRADE 8

2 THE ART OF TRANSPORTATION 12

3 THE ART OF WARFARE 18

4 THE TECHNOLOGY OF CONSTRUCTION 22

5 COMMUNICATION AND CALCULATION 29

6 THE TECHNOLOGY OF MEDICINE 34

TIMELINE 42

GLOSSARY 43

FOR MORE INFORMATION 44

FOR FURTHER READING 45

BIBLIOGRAPHY 46

INDEX 47

INTRODUCTION

ROMAN TECHNOLOGY CONQUERS THE WORLD

At its greatest, the ancient Roman Empire stretched from Britain to the Black Sea, from Spain to Syria, and from northern Africa to northern Europe. Roman technology developed roads, bridges, and aqueducts that spanned the empire in the wake of its army's victories. The word "technology" comes from the Greek words *techne*, which means "art" or "craft," and *logos*, which means "word" or "study." "Technology" has come to mean "the use of science and engineering to perform practical tasks." The influence of Rome lingers thousands of years after the passing of the empire in a legacy of writings, buildings, and bridges.

Legend holds that Rome was founded in 753 BC by twin brothers Romulus and Remus. They were said to be the sons of the war god, Mars, and were raised by a wolf. However, archaeological evidence indicates that Rome began as a small settlement among seven hills along the Tiber River on the Italian peninsula in the ninth century BC., The original Romans were farmers who migrated into south Etruria (central Italy) from Latium.

For several centuries, the earliest Romans were ruled by Etruscan kings. An uprising of Romans overthrew King Tarquin in 509 BC and these Romans established a republic. A group of noblemen, the Senate, annually elected two consuls to rule. By the third century BC, Rome ruled

The Romans built the aqueduct in the Plaza del Azoguejo in Segovia, Spain, around the time of Augustus (63 BC–AD 14), the first Roman emperor. Still standing today, the double tier of arches, made of granite blocks and without mortar, channels water into Segovia and is an impressive example of one of the great feats in engineering of the ancient Romans.

This map, with all the names given in Latin, shows the territory under Roman rule near the end of the Roman Republic, around 44 BC.

the entire Italian peninsula and expanded its power throughout the Mediterranean Sea area. The Roman army defeated the Carthaginians and the Greeks to become rulers of the entire Mediterranean.

The republican system reigned until civil wars threatened Rome's stability and power. Julius Caesar (100–44 BC) prevailed over several other generals to rule as dictator for life. After his assassination in 44 BC, his adopted son, Octavius Caesar Augustus, became Rome's first emperor. During Augustus's sovereignty, the Mediterranean basin experienced a period of relative peace and prosperity known as the *Pax Romana* (Roman peace). Emperors reigned for the next 400 years until the western half of the Roman Empire declined and fell apart.

Many of Rome's advances in technology were due to the mighty Roman army. Engineers for the army built roads, bridges, and aqueducts. Doctors worked to keep the troops healthy with medicine and surgery. Generals planned battles and sieges that conquered vast territories and made Rome one of the greatest empires of the ancient world.

Western civilization benefited from the Romans' progress in many fields. The Latin alphabet is still used in many places around the globe. Roman-style architecture can be seen in countries worldwide, including the United States. In fact, many ancient Roman structures still stand in Italy. Medicine throughout the Middle Ages was based on discoveries and writings made by the ancient Romans. The Roman legal system administered a vast empire with a structure that other governments copied for many years to follow.

Although the Romans copied much from the Greeks, they improved and expanded Greek ideas to make them distinctly their own. Few civilizations before or since have influenced the known world as the Roman Empire has.

THE TECHNOLOGY OF AGRICULTURE AND TRADE

The ancient Romans farmed the hills of the Italian peninsula. In the earliest years before Rome was founded in the ninth century BC, their methods were primitive, requiring the use of wooden hoes and plows. These were later developed into iron hoes and iron-tipped plows pulled by oxen. Oxen were among the most valuable of farm animals because they were used to till the ground and to haul goods to market in wheeled carts.

The major crops grown were grains, such as wheat and barley, and fruit, especially olives and grapes. To begin with, these were culti-vated on small one-family farms. Later, in the first century AD, as the city of Rome grew into a metropolis with more than 1,000,000 people, the demand for food was great. Landowners bought up smaller farms and used slaves to cultivate larger and larger areas.

Romans used large grain mills, such as these in the bakery of Popidius Priscus in Pompeii, to grind barley, wheat, and millet into flour. The mill had two parts, a bell-shaped bottom part that fits into an hourglass-shaped upper part, both made from volcanic rock. An animal turned the upper stone, which crushed the grain that was fed into a hopper.

Mills

The Romans processed grains at gristmills. The overshot mill was developed in the first century AD. The Greeks had pioneered the use of gears, but in the overshot mill the Romans perfected the technique of using water to fall over the top of a wheel to turn gears and power a mill. Falling water powered mills that ground grain and cut wood and marble.

The warm climate of the Italian peninsula encouraged the growth of large orchards of olives. Making olive oil was a difficult process. First, the olive's seed had to be separated from the olive in a basin that had two crushing stones, which revolved around the basin without touching the sides. Once the seeds were taken out, the resulting pulp was squeezed in the olive press. Olive oil was skimmed from the juice that flowed out of the

Men are pressing grapes in this Roman floor mosaic in France that dates from the second century AD. Jars placed alongside the vat caught the grape juice as it flowed out from spigots. The pulp that was left in the vat's bottom was next taken to the wine press.

press. Romans used the oil for cooking, lighting, and bathing.

Vineyards

Grapes also grew well in the Italian climate. Vineyards flourished along the rural hillsides of Rome's conquests on the peninsula after the fourth century BC. Slaves harvested the grapes and stomped on them in a vat to bring out the grapes' juices, which flowed into pottery jars. The resulting pulp was further squeezed in wine presses that were large rush containers. Slaves cranked down a large wooden beam to extract more juices. The grape juice was placed in pottery jars to ferment into wine. Wine and olive oil were stored in large pottery jars called amphorae that stored the precious liquids for later use or transport to the market.

Trade

As the city of Rome grew, along with other cities of the empire, trade became important. Food, wine, olive oil, cloth, and other commodities were traded and transported about the empire. Good roads and harbors constructed by Roman army engineers enabled the transport of these valuable goods.

In the early years of the Roman Republic, farmers and merchants bartered goods and services. Around 290 BC, the Romans began minting coins after they had seen the ones used in Greek colonies in central and southern Italy. These coins first were imprinted with the image of a god or goddess. The copper as, gold aureus, and silver denarius represented differing values. In the first and second centuries AD, when the empire was at its strongest, Roman emperors ordered coins with their own likenesses on them to be minted.

Peace, imposed and policed by the great Roman army, made trade possible throughout the entire Mediterranean region and beyond. Large ships plied the seas while carts traveled well-built roads to carry the best of the empire's goods to Rome and other great cities of the ancient world.

THE ART OF TRANSPORTATION

"All roads lead to Rome." This old saying refers to ancient Rome's vast network of roads that reached throughout the empire. More than 50,000 miles (80,467 kilometers) of roads extended from Rome to the farthest provinces. Army engineers often designed and constructed roads as a means to swiftly move army legions from place to place and to keep them supplied. Merchants followed the movement of the armies, thus promoting the growth of trade and commerce.

Roads

The city of Rome had about 55 miles (89 km) of paved streets. Most of these streets were from 16 to 21 feet (from 4.8 to 6.4 meters) wide and had gutters along the sides to drain rainwater and sewage into the underground sewers.

The roads that radiated from Rome were solidly built. Engineers carefully planned the routes of the roads using surveying instruments such as the *groma*, which had also been used by the Egyptians and Greeks. A groma estimated straight lines and was used as a sighting device when building roads, buildings, and aqueducts. Made of a stand with a wooden crossbar, a groma had weights that hung from the ends of each bar to ensure that the device was placed perpendicular to the ground.

Roman roads ran along mostly straight lines with few curves. The Via Appia is one of the better-known roads of Rome. The Via Flaminia left Rome to traverse the Italian peninsula to the east central coast and then north to the foothills of the Alps. Many other roads radiated from Rome like spokes from a wheel's hub. The Via Salaria, Via Clodia, Via Caecilia, and Via Latina were some of the major roads that originated in Rome to spread out to other parts of the empire.

In road building the first step was digging a large trench about 3 feet (1 m) deep. This trench was filled with a layer of large stones, a layer of gravel, then a layer of sand and flint,

A groma, such as the one pictured here from the first century BC, was used by surveyors and architects as a cross-sight tool for laying out straight lines and right angles when planning the foundations of buildings and roads. A vertical staff was used to hold the weighted plumb lines, which helped in sighting a selected point.

before being paved with flat stones. The surface of the road was not level, but was curved upward by adding a camber, or slightly arched surface. This arched surface allowed water to drain toward ditches on each side of the road. The water had to be quickly

VIA APPIA, THE APPIAN WAY

The Via Appia, or Appian Way, is the oldest road of the early Roman Republic. It was begun by the censor, Appius Claudius Caecus, in 312 BC, and took more than 150 years to complete. In its final form, it passed from the Servian Wall at Rome, 350 miles (563 km) to Brundisium on the Adriatic Sea. The road is extremely straight from Rome to Terracina, even though it passes through swampy land and over steep grades. More than 900 years after the road was built, the historian Procopius wrote that the Appian Way was one of the greatest sights in the world.

This Roman carving, called a relief, shows builders working on a road from around the first century AD. The surface of many Roman roads that were traveled by chariots had six-sided capstones called pavers to enable the wheeled vehicles to move over them quickly.

drained away to keep puddles from forming. Water puddles could freeze and damage the pavement.

Roads were sometimes built up with earth banks called *aggers* instead of being dug into the ground. Dirt was piled up, and the road was built on top of the agger. Large stones were placed on top of the agger. These roads, which could be up to 50 feet (15 m) wide and 5 feet (1.5 m) high, were larger than other roads. The aggers were sometimes used as dividing lines between territories to make boundaries clear.

Bridges

When Roman road builders came to rivers or steep valleys, they constructed bridges or viaducts. The ancient Romans were very adept at building bridges. The ends of the bridge, called abutments, were built on each side, and piers were situated in the middle. The abutments and piers carried most of the bridge's weight. Then arches, made of brick or stone, were built to support the bridge. An arch extended from an abutment to a pier, and another arch went from a pier to an abutment to span the river or valley. This method of construction allowed Roman roads to cross natural obstacles in a straight, level way.

Many ancient Roman bridges still stand and are in use throughout Europe today. Two distinctive examples are the bridge at Alcantara (built across the Tagus River in Spain in AD 106) and the Pons Fabricius (built across the Tiber River in Rome in 62 BC).

The Pons Fabricius (Fabrician Bridge) was built across the Tiber in Rome in 62 BC. In addition to wood, Roman bridges were also made from granite, brick, and concrete.

Ships

In addition to ground transportation, sea travel on sailing ships was used throughout the Roman Empire. In the early years of the Roman Republic (sixth century BC), small cargo ships carried grain and other goods from port to port along the coastline. These ships had one large square sail on one mast and were steered by a smaller sail and two steering oars.

As Rome developed trade throughout the Mediterranean, larger and larger ships were constructed. Ships up to 175 feet (53.4 m) in length and 45 feet (14 m) in width could carry more than 100 tons (90.7 metric tons). There are even a few examples of ships that could carry as much as 600 tons (544.3 t). Cargo ships could travel up to 4 miles per hour (6.4 km/h).

Warships were developed after the Greeks' design for the trireme. These warships had several rows of oars and a large square sail. Wind power moved the ship from place to place, but men powered the oars in battle. The ships' bow came to a sharp point and was used to ram enemy ships. A large flat deck carried about 120 soldiers who would attack enemy ships with arrows and spears.

Some warships had a bridge on hinges to move soldiers to the enemy ship where they engaged in hand-to-hand combat. Other ships were armed with catapults that could shoot large spears or flaming arrows toward the enemy.

Harbors

Roman ports welcomed ships from the Mediterranean trade routes. Most ports were natural harbors, but as larger ships were built, deeper harbors had to be constructed. Ostia, the town that served as the port city of Rome, had human-made harbor works as did nearby Portus. Harbor walls protected the ships from the sea while they were docked. Even at natural harbors, docks and ramps had to be constructed to assist the loading and unloading of cargo ships.

Lighthouses

At harbors and other natural points, lighthouses were constructed to aid in navigation. The most famous lighthouse of the ancient world was the Greeks' Pharos of Alexandria, built around 280 BC, which is one of the

J. M. Gassend painted this modern fresco, or wall painting, showing a reconstruction of how Carthage's harbor looked in the third century BC during the time of Hannibal. Town planning included a basin enclosed by fortified walls, docks for merchants' and navy ships, warehouses, colonnaded public buildings, baths, stone roads, temples, private houses with atria, an amphitheater, and the town forum, a large paved rectangular space.

Seven Wonders of the Ancient World. It stood more than 350 feet (110 m) high and used polished bronze mirrors to reflect light that could be seen many miles out to sea. It was used as a model for Roman lighthouses such as those at Dover, England, and La Coruña, Spain, which can still be seen today. These have original Roman stonework that has survived the centuries to show how Romans constructed lighthouses. Due to their mastery of masonry, Romans were able to construct thick, large walls at the base of the lighthouse that could support the weight of the higher, upper portions.

THE ART OF WARFARE

The Roman army gave Rome dominance in the ancient world. Roman legions conquered countries, tribes, and provinces, all of which eventually became part of the Roman Empire. The Roman army played an important role in the development of the empire both internally and externally. Even Roman politics were influenced by the army due to a soldier's allegiance to his commander. Julius Caesar used his legions to dominate the republic and to declare himself dictator for life. Later, emperors utilized the army to rule Rome and the whole empire.

The ancient world saw the most disciplined army ever in Rome's legions. In the earliest years, landowners served as soldiers in the army who fought short wars against nearby towns or tribes. As Rome's territory and influence increased, the army organized to better defend and expand Rome's power. In 100 BC, General Gaius Marius organized the army into units of foot soldiers called legions. A legion was made of ten cohorts, which had six to eight centuries of eighty men each. A century had ten *contuberni* made of eight men who tented together. With this type of organization, legions had between 4,800 and 6,000 men.

Weapons

The legionnare, a Roman soldier, was very well equipped, often carrying 60 to 100 pounds (27.2 to 45.4 kg) of armor, weapons, and tools. The legionnare carried from three to fourteen days' worth of food, a piece of rope or leather, a shovel, a pickax, a sickle, a wicker basket, and a saw. Because the men carried so much equipment, they earned, in the late second century BC, the nickname Marius's Mules after General Marius, who required his soldiers to lug all this equipment.

Each man wore a metal helmet in addition to body armor made of leather and strips of metal—bronze or steel—to protect his chest and abdomen. The soldier also carried a large curved shield to surround his body. The shield (scutum), made of wood, leather, and metal, protected the individual soldier or could be

Roman legionnaires are depicted in this relief from the Column of Marcus Aurelius in Rome, which was made in the second century AD. The legionnaires are using the formation called a testudo, in which they raise their shields above their heads for protection against enemies' arrows.

linked to protect a group of soldiers. Legionnaires on the first rank held their shields before them to present a wall to the enemy. Following ranks raised their shields overhead to protect the soldiers from falling arrows. This formation was called a testudo, which means "tortoise."

The average legionnare carried several weapons into battle. The *gladius*, a short sword of about 22 inches (55.9 centimeters) long and 2 inches (5.1 cm) wide, was a double-bladed thrusting weapon. A smaller dagger called a *pugio* was worn on the left side opposite the gladius on the right. The pugio, which was about 7 to 11 inches (17.8 to 27.9 cm) long and 2 inches (5.1 cm) wide, was a secondary weapon used for stabbing when other weapons were lost.

Each soldier also used a *pilum*, a 7-foot-long (2.1 m) spear, with a hardened iron point and a shaft of softer metal. When the pilum struck an enemy's shield, the point penetrated, but the softer metal bent when someone tried to remove it. This caused the pilum to be stuck in the enemy's shield. The pilum was usually thrown at the enemy just before the armies collided in hand-to-hand combat. Each legionnare carried two pila, which were thrown at the enemy in volley.

Artillery

Roman armies also had artillery made up of bows and arrows and large catapults. Archers shot arrows over the first ranks to rain down on the enemy. Larger machines called catapults hurled long spears, boulders, and flaming balls at the enemy army or fortification. The catapult, or onager, which means "wild ass," could kick rocks of up to 150 pounds (68 kg) about 1,600 feet (488 m) to smash fort walls and enemy ranks.

Forts and Sieges

The Romans were experts in fortifications used for defense and for quartering Roman soldiers during the winter or times of peace. Fortifications had strong stone or wood walls, usually with a protecting ditch surrounding them. The soldiers constructed the stone walls 15 feet (4.6 m) high and 3 feet (1 m) thick. Towers and turrets, stationed at various points along the wall and at corners, offered vantage points for defending soldiers to shoot arrows, hurl spears, or throw rocks onto attacking forces.

Romans soldiers are depicted besieging a town in this Italian engraving from the nineteenth century. Some of the weapons represented are the Roman catapult (onager), which fired rocks, a giant crossbow (ballista), and siege towers with battering rams.

Roman legions were also masters at the siege of enemy forts. Soldiers constructed siege towers taller than the city walls. Other soldiers pushed the siege towers to the city walls to allow still other soldiers to climb over the fortifications. Battering rams, which were large tree trunks with an iron ram's head on the end, were mounted on wheels to bash holes in city gates and walls, allowing soldiers to rush into the city.

Romans mastered the technology of warfare to conquer a large part of the ancient world. Their ability to move huge armies over well-built roads to far-flung territories with superior equipment forged an enormous empire.

THE TECHNOLOGY OF CONSTRUCTION

The Romans designed and built great structures both large and small. Roman architecture borrowed freely from Greek and Etruscan influences. Romans constructed temples and theaters modeled after those they observed during their conquest of the Italian peninsula and Greek colonies. Imitation was not enough for the Romans who used creativity and ingenuity to improve the designs of others; Romans even made some great innovations of their own. The invention of concrete allowed the Romans to make advances in the construction of buildings and public works. Roman engineering produced many impressive structures in Rome and in numerous other cities of the empire. The fact that many Roman buildings are still standing throughout Europe today is a testament to the quality of ancient Roman building technology.

The barrel-vaulted room of the Flavian Amphitheater in Pozzuoli, Italy, was first begun under Emperor Nero but finished by Emperor Vespasian in AD 79. Concrete vaulting by the Romans made it possible for architects to construct the large-scale interiors of amphitheaters and baths.

Roman Building Innovations

In the second century BC, Roman builders developed concrete, a mortar mixture of limestone, volcanic ash, and stones. Using concrete allowed architects and engineers to construct large buildings with thick walls that could support the weight of a heavy roof. Workers constructed wooden forms into which the concrete was poured. This liquid "rock" hardened into shapes that would have been difficult to sculpt from stone.

The arch, which was most likely invented by the Mesopotamians, was improved by the Romans and applied extensively to buildings,

The interior of the Pantheon in Rome illustrates the Roman achievement of being able to construct a one-room circular building with multiple barrel vaults, called a dome, by using concrete and bricks.

bridges, and aqueducts. Many ancient cultures used post-and-lintel construction with columns and beams. The Romans built some buildings with the post-and-lintel design. The arch began to replace the post-and-lintel design, because arches could bear more weight and span longer distances.

A row of arches formed a vault that could cover a large area that was called a barrel or tunnel vault. Later, two vaults joined at right angles made a cross-vaulted building, which could cover an even larger area and admit more light than the barrel vault because it had four end openings instead of two. Eventually, builders crossed a number of arches over one another to create a dome. The dome formed an enormous covering over a huge square, round, or even octagonal area. The Pantheon, built in Rome by Emperor Hadrian (AD 76–138) between ad 118 and 128, is an outstanding example of concrete and dome construction, and shows the Roman mastery of creating interior space. Concrete allowed the Romans to have a material that was stonelike but that could be formed into necessary shapes.

Ancient Romans used clay heating pipes, such as these in the Casa del Triclinio in Ostia, Italy, to heat villa interiors. This method was also used to heat water and floors in public baths.

Dwellings

Rich Romans built compounds called villas that had a central space (atrium), a bath, a garden, and numerous rooms, such as bedrooms, a dining room, and sitting areas. A central heating system, called a hypocaust, could be added to the first floor of a villa. Piers under the house allowed hot air from a furnace to flow through and warm the floor. This same system was used to heat public baths in the city. Craftsmen decorated the floors of some of the villa's rooms with elaborate mosaics of small colored stones. Frescoes, or paintings done on wet plaster, adorned villa walls. Today, examples of these ways of building and decorating can be seen in the ancient ruins of Pompeii and Herculaneum.

By the first century AD, poorer citizens lived in an *insula*, a large, multistoried (two to seven stories tall) apartment building that covered an entire city block. People lived in small

THE COLOSSEUM

Emperor Titus Flavius Sabinus Vespasian ordered a large oval arena to be built in Rome during his reign. The word "arena" comes from the Roman word for sand and was used to describe the sand that covered the floor of the center of the large amphitheater. The Colosseum could hold 50,000 people. Fights and battles were staged in the 6,000-square-foot (557.4-square-meter) area. Fights between gladiators and animals, gladiators and other gladiators, and animals and other animals thrilled large crowds of Romans. Sometimes the arena's floor, which was made of stone, concrete, and sand, was flooded to provide an artificial lake for mock sea battles with ships. Canvas awnings, worked by former sailors, could be pulled across the seating area to provide shelter from sun or rain.

The Colosseum, built from AD 72 to 80, still stands in downtown Rome as a monument not only to Roman engineering but also to Roman excesses in the gladiatorial contests.

one-room apartments in the upper stories. Shops occupied rooms on the street level. Lavatories for the entire insula were located along the street near the underground sewers. Lead pipes were used to bring the water from the aqueducts that brought the water into the city.

Aqueducts

By the second century AD, the city of Rome had more than 1,000,000 people living in it. The large population required a great amount of water. More than ten aqueducts brought 38,000,000 gallons (143,845,656 liters) of water into Rome each day. Another Roman-built aqueduct, the Pont du Gard in France, carried water 30 miles (48 km) into the city of Nîmes. The Pont du Gard and the double-arched aqueduct in Segovia, Spain, are among the Roman aqueducts that still function today.

Public Buildings

In addition to aqueducts and sewers, ancient Romans built temples and large public buildings. The forum was an open area, usually in the center of a city, where Romans conducted business. In Rome, several large triumphal arches, such as the Arch of Titus, celebrated the victories of emperors against foreign armies. In the first century AD, the emperor Titus Flavius Sabinus Vespasian (AD 9–79) began the construction of the Colosseum near Rome's forum.

Workmen quarried stone for the Colosseum nearly 20 miles (32 km) away. These workmen drilled into the stone, drove wooden wedges into the holes, and soaked the wedges with water, causing them to expand and break the stone. The stones were then trimmed and transported by oxcart to the city. At the work site, the heavy stones were lifted into place by cranes powered by men, ropes, and pulleys. The Romans built more oval amphitheaters like the Colosseum in other parts of the empire.

Augustus Caesar had marble quarried from Carrara more than 230 miles (370 km) north of Rome. According to *Divus Augustus*, a biography written by the Roman historian and biographer Gaius Suetonius Tranquillus (AD circa 69–122), Augustus bragged that he "found Rome a city of brick and left it a city of marble." Augustus and later emperors erected many buildings and monuments of marble to make Rome a glorious city at the center of the empire.

Statues

Artisans used the lost wax method to make bronze statues that adorned the Colosseum, triumphal arches, and other public buildings. In this method, a clay version of the statue was covered with wax. An outer clay covering was added. As the bronze was poured in, the wax melted. A thin bronze shell formed the statue. A large bronze statue of Nero stood near the Colosseum and gave the arena its name, because the statue was colossal.

COMMUNICATION AND CALCULATION

Roman numbers and letters have survived for thousands of years to be in use today. The Roman alphabet, with its twenty-two characters, was modeled after the Greek alphabet. In the Roman alphabet *I* and *J* were represented by the same symbol and *U* and *V* were represented by the same symbol. The letters *W* and *Y* were not part of the alphabet. With only a few modifications, the Roman alphabet is still used in English and many other languages throughout the world.

Writing

The language that the Romans spoke and wrote is known as Latin. Although Latin is not spoken today, it is still alive in various forms. Many languages, such as French, Spanish, Italian, and Romanian, are based on Latin. Many English words are derived from Latin.

This ancient Roman tablet *(top)* is the first "page" from a Roman will that was found near Trawsfynydd, Wales, in the nineteenth century. A portrait *(bottom)* from a fresco in Naples depicts a young Roman girl holding a stylus and some writing tablets.

The Roman Catholic Church uses Latin in liturgy and official documents, as do many universities.

Roman students learned to write with a wooden stylus on a wax tablet. As students practiced on the wax with the stylus, they would use the sharp end of the stylus to form the letters. When the lesson was over, the flat end of the stylus was used to smooth the wax to erase the work. A stylus could be made of wood, reeds, bronze, or ivory.

A stylus dipped in ink, which was made from fine soot mixed with water, was used to write on papyrus or vellum. Papyrus was a kind of paper made of reeds. The wet reeds were placed in layers, pressed together, and then sanded with stones. The papyrus sheets were connected to make rolls called scrolls. Thin animal skins, such as those of goats or lambs, were cleaned to make a durable writing surface called vellum.

Romans loved books and collected them. Wealthy people had books in scroll form at home. However, the emperor and others gathered works together into libraries. The making of a

ROMAN NUMERALS

The Romans devised a system of symbols using seven letters of their alphabet that represented numbers.

I	=	1	C	=	100
V	=	5	D	=	500
X	=	10	M	=	1,000
L	=	50			

Roman numerals were read from left to right. The symbols for the largest number are written on the left. The next largest appears to the right. The numbers are usually added together. For instance, CLV is 155 and MDXII is 1,512. However, when the symbol for a smaller number is to the left of that for a larger one, the smaller number is subtracted. Examples are IV for 4, IX for 9, and MCMXCIX for 1999. Roman numerals are still used today for formal documents, clock faces, and various other applications. A disadvantage to using Roman numerals is that rapid calculations are difficult to perform.

book was a long, difficult process. After making the papyrus, scribes had to write every word by hand on every copy. By the fourth century AD, scrolls began to be replaced by stacks of papyrus or vellum that were bound together. This booklike volume was known as a codex. Many of these codices, such as the *Codex Sinaiticus* in the British Library and *Codex Vaticanus* in the Vatican Library, can be seen in museums around the world.

Ancient Roman writers are still read today. The poets Ovid (43 BC–AD 17), Horace (65–8 BC), and Virgil (70–19 BC) set standards that poets imitated for centuries. Pliny the Elder (circa AD 23–79), Pliny the Younger (AD 62–113), and Livy (59 BC–AD 17) chronicled life and history through their writings that continue to give insight into Roman daily life.

The Calendar

Keeping an accurate calendar was important for many reasons, especially in calculating the observance of religious festivals. The early Roman calendar had difficulties because of a superstition that even numbers were unlucky. Eleven of the twelve months had either twenty-nine or thirty-one days with February having twenty-eight. This made the year 355 days long. So, every other year, the month of Mercedonius, with twenty-two or twenty-three days, was added to the year. (Mercedonius takes its name from the Latin word *merces* for "wages" because workers were usually paid at this time of the year.) Even with this correction, the calendar became more and more inaccurate.

In 45 BC, Julius Caesar consulted with the astronomer Sosigenes about the true length of the year. Sosigenes calculated the year to be 365 days and 6 hours long. The system of having a leap year with an extra day every four years was instituted by Julius Caesar, who decreed a special year of 445 days to bring the calendar back in line with the seasons. Even with this Julian calendar, as it was called, the year was still 11 minutes and 14 seconds off. In the sixteenth century, the present system, the Gregorian calendar, was put into effect.

The names and order of the months that are used today come from the Roman calendar. In the early Roman calendar (seventh century BC) there were only ten months, with March being the first month of the year. Later, January, named for the two-faced Roman god, Janus, was added and became the first month and February was added, too. Later still, the month Quintilis (fifth month) was renamed July after Julius Caesar and Sextilis (sixth month) was renamed August after Caesar Augustus, and these were added to the year to make the 365-day year that we now use. This two-month addition made the seventh month, September, the ninth month, and the eighth month, October, became the tenth month, and so on.

Even the names of the sevens days of the week we use today have their

This Roman (Julian) calendar indicates years, months, and days of the week with pegs. The Roman zodiac appears within the circle and Roman numerals can be seen along the left and right sides of the stone.

origins from the Romans and their mythology. The days were named after celestial bodies: Saturn's day, the sun's day, the moon's day, and so on. In English, the names of the Norse gods Tiu, Woden, Thor, and Freya for Tuesday, Wednesday, Thursday, and Friday, replaced Mars, Mercury, Jupiter, and Venus.

Roman writing, numerals, and the calendar are still used in many countries throughout the world, including the United States and Europe. The Roman technology of calculating time and recording history has been invaluable down through the centuries and shows the great influence of the ancient world on our own life and times.

THE TECHNOLOGY OF MEDICINE

In medicine, the Romans learned from the ancient Greeks. The writings of Hippocrates (circa 460–377 BC) shaped rational Roman medicine. Like the Greeks, the Romans believed that illness and disease could be cured by the gods. Temples to Aesculapius and his daughter, Hygieia, the goddess of healing, stood in many cities throughout the Roman Empire. The most famous of these stood on an island in the Tiber River in Rome. The sick prayed and slept at the temple for healing, which was delivered in the form of dreams. People often made votive offerings in the shape of the diseased body part, such as a leg, an ear, or a hand, formed out of iron or pottery. People who had been healed left these votives as offerings to the gods.

Healing herbs, such as fennel, elecampane, sage, and rosemary, soothed and cured many people of illnesses from indigestion to

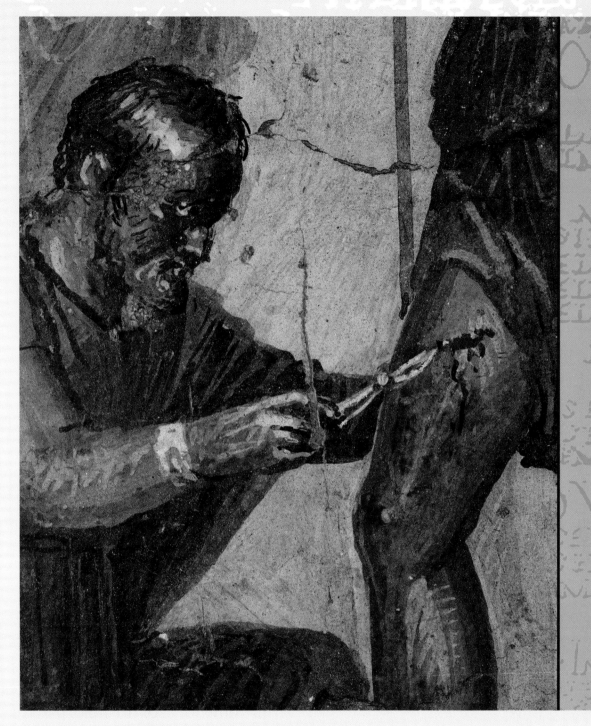

A detail from a fresco in the Casa di Sirico, Pompeii, which dates from the first century AD, shows the legendary hero Aeneas having an arrowhead surgically removed by a doctor. The surgeon is depicted using forceps. Roman armies were the first to use physicians on the battlefield.

headaches. Physicians, such as Asclepiades (124–40 BC) and Galen (AD circa 129–199) studied the effects of various plants on diseases. Herbs grown in small gardens were dried and ground into powders that were then mixed with wine or water for the patient to drink. Soldiers were fed a daily ration of garlic to keep them healthy. Pliny the Elder recorded about forty cures in which mustard was the main ingredient. The cures ranged from stomachaches to breathing difficulties.

Physicians in the army worked to keep soldiers healthy. They attempted to keep the military camps and forts clean and free of disease. It is thought that Julius Caesar first brought doctors onto the battlefield to tend to the wounded. These doctors learned much about the human body as they tried to help soldiers wounded in battle. Sometimes surgery was required to set broken bones, repair cut muscle and blood vessels, or remove arrows or spear points.

Surgery

Roman physicians who worked in the army contributed to improved surgical techniques. They developed tools of iron and bronze to assist the surgeons in their work. Scalpels were made of iron, bronze, or steel and were used to make incisions. Metal hooks and probes helped the doctor push aside tissue during surgery. The Romans understood that sometimes limbs had to be amputated to prevent infection or gangrene. This was a common practice by the time Emperor Augustus elevated the status of physicians to keep his army healthy. Bone saws could cut a bone for amputation and the scalpels were used to cut away tissue and muscle.

Surgery was a painful and dangerous procedure and was probably performed only as a last resort. At the time, no anesthetics were available to numb the pain. Patients drank wine to relieve some of their pain and suffering during operations. Most surgeons repaired hernias and removed tumors, but more complicated types of surgeries required physicians of great skill. Bronze tubes were used as catheters and specula (instruments used to hold parts of the body open) for internal exams.

It is known that the ancient Romans performed brain surgery. The Romans used a drill to bore a hole in the skull to relieve pressure and cure headaches. Interestingly, this brain

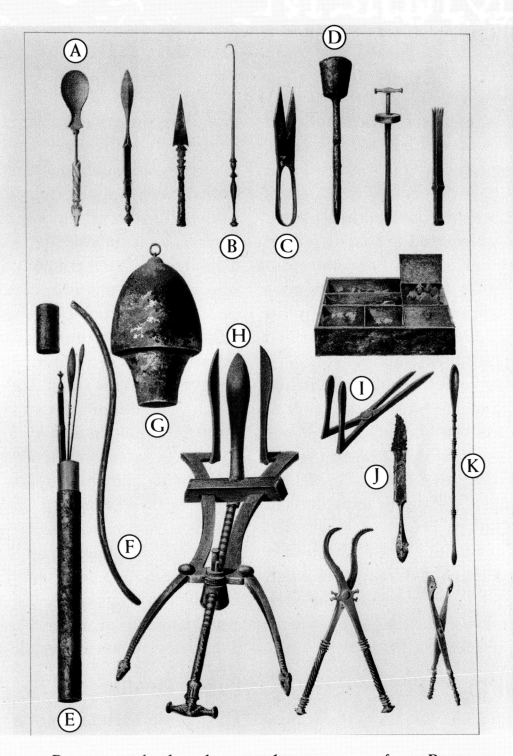

Ancient Roman medical and surgical instruments from Pompeii are shown in this nineteenth-century illustration. Some of the instruments included are: (top row) a spoon (A), hook (B), surgical scissors (C), and clyster (D, used for administering enemas); (bottom row) a portable probe case (E), catheter (F), cupping vessel for bloodletting (G), speculum (H), bone forceps (I), scalpel (J), and spatula (K).

surgery could be successful and patients had a high survival rate. Other ancient cultures carried out brain surgeries, called trepanation, that cut away the bone of the skull, but the Romans seemed to have improved on these methods. In first century AD Rome, Aulus Cornelius Celsus conducted delicate brain surgeries. In his writings *On Medicine*, he described symptoms of brain injuries in detail.

Another delicate surgery executed by the Romans involved the removal of cataracts, the clouding of the lenses in the eye. A thin, hollow needle was pushed into the eye to break up the cataract. The pieces of the broken cataract were then suctioned out through the hollow tube of the needle. Although this removed the cataract, nothing was used to replace the eye's lens, and so the patient's vision became blurred.

Childbirth

Normally, a midwife assisted a woman with childbirth. Midwives were women trained in the healing arts of herb medicine and birthing. Soranus (AD 98–138) wrote of many procedures for midwives and childbirth. He spoke of using olive oil rubdowns to ease the pain of childbirth and any aftereffects. Midwives rather than physicians attended to women at most births, but especially helped in difficult births that could result in the mother's or infant's death.

Roman law required that a woman who died in childbirth could not be buried until the baby had been delivered. The procedure known as the Caesarean section, an operation to remove the baby from the mother, which is quite common and safe today, was first developed to deliver the baby after the mother's death so that both could be properly buried. Later, by the fourth or fifth century AD, this procedure was used as a last resort to save a baby's life. The law required that this procedure not be done until the tenth month of pregnancy. Usually the mother would not survive the operation, but sometimes the child did.

Public Health

The word "hygiene" means "cleanliness," and comes from the name for the Roman goddess of healing, Hygieia. The Romans understood the connection between filth and disease and worked to have cleaner cities. Rome itself had an intricate sewer system that

This view from Hadrian's Baths in Leptis Magna, Libya, shows the communal latrines (toilets), which were constructed around AD 127. The seats were made from marble, and water flowed in an open channel in the floor.

could carry human waste into the streams and rivers. Stone and dirt gutters along the streets collected rainwater and waste that was discarded in the streets. These gutters emptied into underground sewers that ran throughout the city. The Cloaca Maxima, which can still be found in some parts of Rome today, was a sewer begun before the days of the Roman Republic during the rule of the Tarquins in the sixth century BC.

Public and private baths offered Romans the opportunity to bathe and stay healthy. Some of these baths were large buildings, such as the Baths of Caracalla and the Baths of Diocletian, with big pools of water. Wood furnaces heated the water and the floors of the baths. The laconium was the hottest room of all, and was usually used by older or infirm people. A tub of boiling water in the center of the laconium kept the room filled with steam.

The caldarium had a large pool of hot water for people to sit in. The Romans believed that sweating purged the body of illness and fluids

The Romans used natural hot springs for the baths at Bath, England. The cure-seeking bathers descended steps into the pool, which is lined with forty-five sheets of lead, and enjoyed the hot springs for their helpful benefits.

that caused disease. Next was the tepidarium with warm water in a smaller pool. The coldest water was in the frigidarium, allowing people to swim about in frigid waters. A public bath usually had a yard or large room for exercising, wrestling, and other sports.

There were large public baths, but the richest people had private baths at their homes or villas. These private baths were smaller and naturally did not have the full range of rooms found in the larger public baths. But they did have the frigidarium, tepidarium, and caldarium.

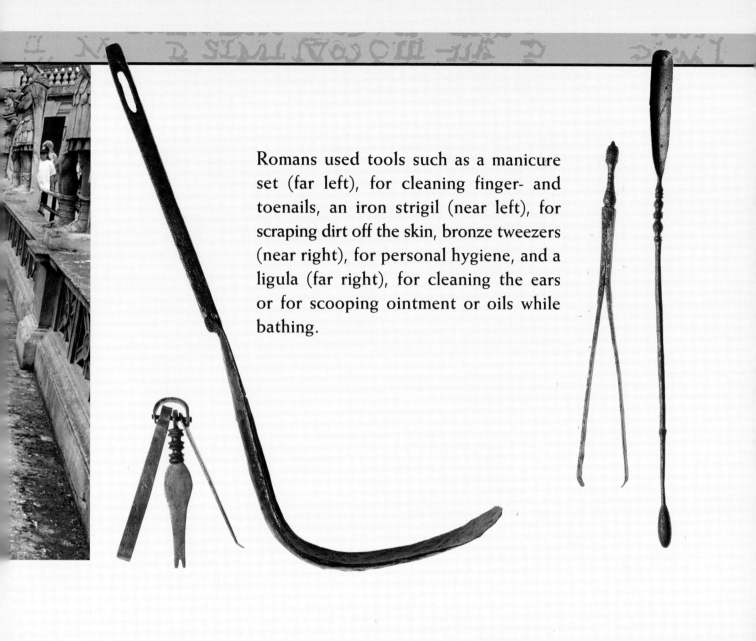

Romans used tools such as a manicure set (far left), for cleaning finger- and toenails, an iron strigil (near left), for scraping dirt off the skin, bronze tweezers (near right), for personal hygiene, and a ligula (far right), for cleaning the ears or for scooping ointment or oils while bathing.

The Romans did not use soap, but instead massaged oil into their bodies. The olive oil would cause dirt in the skin to rise to the surface. Strigils, scrapers of metal, wood, or bone, were then used to scrape off the sweat and dirt.

Many advances were made in medicine and public health by the Romans. Galen, who became physician for Emperor Marcus Aurelius's son in Rome in the first century AD, wrote of his careful observations on medicine in works such as *On the Uses of the Parts of the Body of Man*. He achieved great distinction in Rome for his practice of medicine.

TIMELINE

509 BC	Romans form a republic.
280 BC	Italian peninsula is united under Roman rule.
264–202 BC	Rome defeats Carthage.
147 BC	Rome conquers Greece.
AD 27	Construction of the Pantheon begins.
AD 43	Rome invades Britain.
AD 49	Julius Caesar rules Rome.
AD 72	Construction of the Colosseum begins.
AD 79	Mount Vesuvius destroys the towns of Pompeii and Herculaneum.
AD 395	Roman Empire is divided.
AD 410	Visigoths capture Rome.
AD 455	Vandals sack Rome.
AD 476	Western Roman Empire falls.

GLOSSARY

abutment The end part of a bridge that holds most of the weight of the structure.

amphorae Large, two-handled pottery jars used for storing and transporting goods.

aqueduct A structure for supplying water to an area or city for public and private use.

archaeologist One who studies ancient civilizations by analyzing its objects.

contuberni Tent groups, which consisted of eight men in each contubernium.

Etruscan Inhabitants of ancient Italy before the rise of the Roman Republic.

gladius A short sword used by Roman soldiers in close combat.

insula Multistoried apartment building with shops on the ground level with smaller rooms on the upper levels that were inhabited by poor Romans.

legion Largest unit in the Roman army.

legionnaire A Roman soldier.

onager A catapult that threw large objects long distances.

pilum A 7-foot-long (2 m) spear carried by Roman soldiers.

pugio A small dagger carried by Roman soldiers for close combat.

sovereignty Supreme power or rule.

stylus Writing tool made of bone, metal, or wood.

tablet Wooden boards coated with wax and used for writing.

testudo A cover formed by the overlapping shields of besiegers and held over their heads.

villa A compound that served as a home for wealthy Romans.

FOR MORE INFORMATION

The Archaeological Institute of America
Boston University
656 Beacon Street
Boston, MA 02215
(617) 353-9361
Web site: http://www.archeaological.org

Metropolitan Museum of Art
1000 Fifth Avenue
New York, NY 10028
Web site: http://www.metmuseum.org

Ontario Archaeological Society
11099 Bathurst Street
Richmond Hill, ON L4C ON2
Canada
Web site: http://www.ontario
achaeology.on.ca

Royal Ontario Museum
100 Queen's Park

Toronto, ON M5S 2C6
Canada
Web site: http://www.rom.on.ca

Smithsonian Institution
    Information Center
1000 Jefferson Drive SW
Washington, DC 20560-0010
(202) 357-2700
Web site: http://www.si.edu

Web Sites

Due to the changing nature of Internet links, the Rosen Publishing Group, Inc., has developed an online list of Web sites related to the subject of this book. This site is updated regularly. Please use this link to access the list:

http://www.rosenlinks.com/taw/tear

FOR FURTHER READING

Chisholm, Jane. *Living in Roman Times.*
London, England: Usborne
Publishing, Ltd., 1982.

James, Simon. *Ancient Rome.* London,
England: Dorling Kindersley, 2000.

Jovinelly, Joann, and Jason Netelkos.
The Crafts and Culture of the Romans. New
York, NY: Rosen Publishing, 2002.

Kerr, Daisy. *Ancient Romans.* New York,
NY: Franklin Watts, 1996.

MacDonald, Fiona, and Mark Bergin.
Inside Story The Roman Colosseum.
New York, NY: Peter Bedrick
Books, 1998.

Malam, John. *Myths and Civilization of the
Ancient Romans.* New York, NY: Peter
Bedrick Books, 1999.

Marks, Anthony, and Graham Tingay.
The Romans. Tulsa, OK: Educational
Development Corporation, 2001.

Morley, Jacqueline, and John James.
Inside Story: A Roman Villa. New York,
NY: Peter Bedrick Books, 1998.

Nardo, Don. *Greek and Roman Science.*
(World History Series) San Diego,
CA: Lucent Books, 1998.

Woods, Michael, and Mary B. Woods.
Ancient Construction: From Tents to Towers.
(Ancient Technology). Minneapolis,
MN: Runestone Press, 2000.

Woods, Michael, and Mary B. Woods.
Ancient Warfare: From Clubs to Catapults
(Ancient Technology). Minneapolis,
MN: Runestone Press, 2000.

BIBLIOGRAPHY

Daniels, Patricia S., and Stephen G. Hyslop. *Almanac of World History*. Washington, DC: National Geographic Society, 2003.

Carcopino, Jerome. *Daily Life in Ancient Rome*. New Haven, CT: Yale University Press, 1968.

Chisholm, Jane. *Living in Roman Times*. London, England: Usborne Publishing, Ltd., 1982.

Goldsworthy, Adrian. *Roman Warfare*. London, England: Cassell & Co., 2000.

Hicks, Peter. *The Romans*. New York, NY: Thomson Learning, 1994.

James, Simon. *Ancient Rome*. London, England: Dorling Kindersley, 2000.

Jovinelly, Joann, and Jason Netelkos. *The Crafts and Culture of the Romans*. New York, NY: Rosen Publishing, 2002.

Kerr, Daisy. *Ancient Romans*. New York, NY: Franklin Watts, 1996.

MacDonald, Fiona, and Mark Bergin. *Inside Story: The Roman Colosseum*. New York, NY: Peter Bedrick Books, 1998.

Malam, John. *Myths and Civilization of the Ancient Romans*. New York, NY: Peter Bedrick Books, 1999.

Marks, Anthony, and Graham Tingay. *The Romans*. Tulsa, OK: Educational Development Corporation, 2001.

Morley, Jacqueline, and John James. *Inside Story: A Roman Villa*. New York, NY: Peter Bedrick Books, 1998.

Quennell, Peter. *The Colosseum*. New York, NY: Newsweek, 1971.

Tunis, Edwin. *Weapons: A Pictorial History*. New York, NY: World Publishing, 1972.

INDEX

A

alphabet, 7, 29
apartment building, 25
aqueducts, 5, 13, 27
arch(es), 15, 23–24, 27, 28
army
   and medicine, 7, 36
   organization of, 18–19
   and trade, 11
   and transportation, 6–7, 12
Asclepiades, 34–36
Augustus, Octavius Caesar, 6, 27, 32, 36
Aurelius, Marcus, 41

B

bath(s), 25, 39–40
books, making of, 30–31
bridges, construction of, 15

C

Caesar, Julius, 6, 18, 32, 36
Caesarean section, 38
calendar, 32–33
childbirth, 38
Colosseum, 26, 28
concrete, 22, 23, 24, 26

D

dwellings, 25–27

E

Etruria/Etruscan, 5, 22

F

forts, 20–21

G

Galen, 34–36, 41
gladiators, 26
Greek(s), 6, 7, 11, 16, 22, 29, 34
groma, 13

H

Hadrian, 24
harbors, human-made, 11, 16
herb(s), 34, 36, 38
Hippocrates, 34
Horace, 31

L

Latin, 7, 29–30
lighthouses, 16–17
Livy, 32

M

Marius, Gaius, 19
medicine, gods and, 34, 38
mills, 9

O

olive oil, 9, 11, 38, 40

P

Pantheon, 24
papyrus, 30, 31
Pax Romana (Roman peace), 6

Pharos of Alexandria, 16
Pliny the Elder, 31, 36
Pliny the Younger, 31
public health, 38–41

R
roads, construction of, 12–15
Roman Empire
    history of, 5–6
    legal system of, 7, 38
    modern influence of, 5, 7, 29, 33
    territory of, 5, 6
Roman numbers/numerals, 29, 31, 33

S
sewer(s), 12, 27, 38–39
ships, 11, 16
surgery, 36–38

V
Vespasian, Titus Flavius
    Sabinus, 26, 27
Via Appia, 13, 14

W
weapons and armor, 19–20
writing utensils, 30

About the Author

Charles W. Maynard is a writer who lives in Jonesborough, Tennessee. He has a great interest in ancient Greece and Rome, born out of his study of Latin, Greek, and Hebrew. He is a graduate of Emory & Henry College and Emory University, and he continues to be fascinated with the history, myths, and technology of the ancient world.

Photo Credits

Cover The Art Archive/Bibliothèque des Arts Décoratifs Paris/Dagli Orti; cover (inset) Scala/Art Resource, NY; p. 4 Plaza del Azoguejo, Segovia, Spain/Bridgeman Art Library; p. 6 Originally published in Historical Atlas of the World, © J. W. Cappelens Forlag A/S, Oslo, 1962. Maps by Berit Lie. Used with permission of J.W. Cappelens Forlag; p. 9 © Erich Lessing/ Art Resource, NY; p. 10 Réunion des Musées Nationaux/Art Resource, NY; p.13 © SSPL/The Image Works; p. 14 Museo della Civiltà Romana, Rome, Italy/Bridgeman Art Library; p.15 Scala/Art Resource, NY; p. 17 The Art Archive/Museum of Carthage/Dagli Orti; p. 19 © 2005 Roger-Viollet/ Topham/The Image Works; p. 21 © The Bridgeman Art Library; p. 23 © Mimmo Jodice/ Corbis; p. 24 © Joe Carini/The Image Works; p. 25 Scala/Art Resource, NY; p. 26 © V & W/ The Image Works; p. 30 (top) © National Museum of Wales; p. 30 (bottom) Museo e Gallerie Nazionali di Capodimonte, Naples, Italy, Lauros/Giraudon/ Bridgeman Art Library; p. 33 © AAAC/Topham/The Image Works; p. 35 Erich Lessing/Art Resource, NY; p. 37 The Art Archive/ Bibliothèque des Arts Décoratifs Paris/Dagli Orti; p. 39 Leptis Magna, Libya, Ali Meyer/Bridgeman Art Library; p. 40–41 © Lee Snider/The Image Works; p. 41 Museum of London, England/Bridgeman Art Library.

Editor: Kathy Kuhtz Campbell
Designer: Evelyn Horovicz
Photo Researcher: Jeffrey Wendt